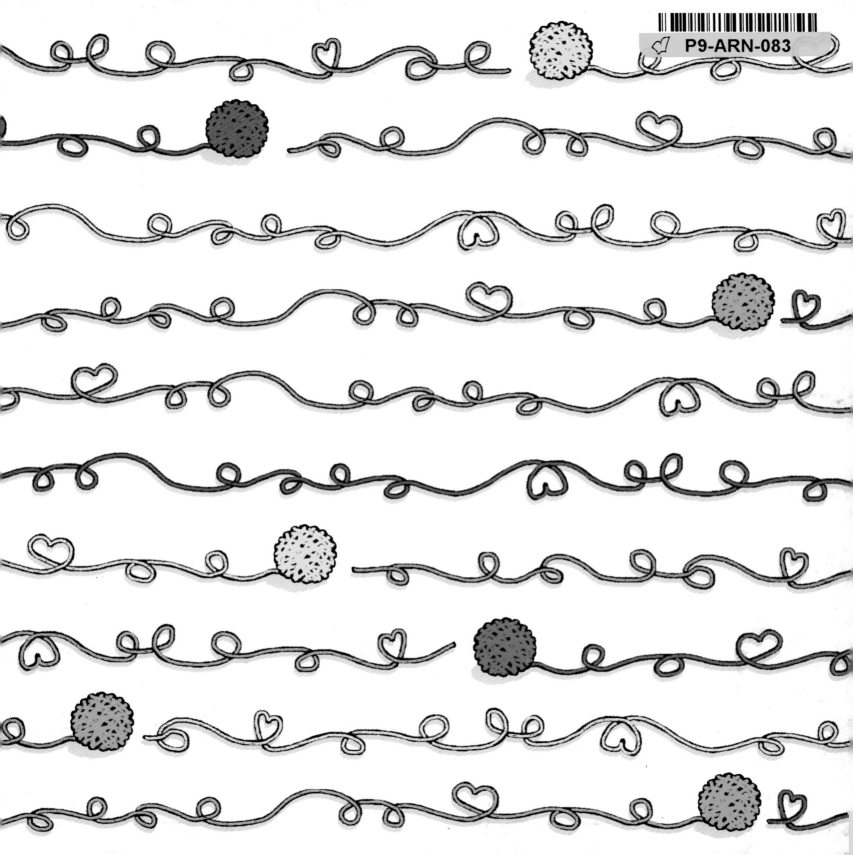

For Umma, whose love knows no bounds

First published in the United States of America in December 2013
by Walker Books for Young Readers, an imprint of Bloomsbury Publishing, Inc.
www.bloomsbury.com

For information about permission to reproduce selections from this book, write to
Permissions, Walker BFYR, 1385 Broadway, New York, New York 10018
Bloomsbury books may be purchased for business or promotional use. For information on bulk purchases
please contact Macmillan Corporate and Premium Sales Department at specialmarkets@macmillan.com

Library of Congress Cataloging-in-Publication Data
Yoon, Salina.
Penguin in love / Salina Yoon.
pages   cm
Summary: One day, Penguin goes looking for love and finds, instead, a mitten, but as he tries to locate the
mitten's owner, he knits his way through a blizzard to an unexpected meeting.
ISBN 978-0-8027-3600-0 (hardcover) • ISBN 978-0-8027-3601-7 (reinforced)
[1. Penguins—Fiction. 2. Knitting—Fiction. 3. Love—Fiction.] I. Title.
PZ7.Y817Pfm 2013   [E]—dc23   2013002847

Art created digitally using Adobe Photoshop
Typeset in Maiandra
Book design by Nicole Gastonguay

Printed in China by C&C Offset Printing Co., Ltd., Shenzhen, Guangdong
1 3 5 7 9 10 8 6 4 2 (hardcover)
1 3 5 7 9 10 8 6 4 2 (reinforced)

All papers used by Bloomsbury Publishing, Inc., are natural, recyclable products
made from wood grown in well-managed forests. The manufacturing processes
conform to the environmental regulations of the country of origin.

Penguin in Love

Salina Yoon

WALKER BOOKS FOR YOUNG READERS
AN IMPRINT OF BLOOMSBURY
NEW YORK   LONDON   NEW DELHI   SYDNEY

One day, Penguin was
looking for love.

Instead, he found . . .

. . . a mitten.

It was a mystery.

Penguin asked Grandpa if it was his.

"No, Penguin. I like to wear hats."

Penguin searched for its owner.

Emily was missing a bead, but not a mitten.

Isabelle was missing a slipper, but not a mitten.

Oliver was missing the sun, but not a mitten.

Penguin wondered who had knitted such a fine mitten.

Meanwhile, Penguin's friend
Bootsy was busy knitting cozies.

These snout cozies
will keep you toasty.

Knitting warmed her lonely heart.

Penguin was busy knitting, too.

Just then, a couple of puffins
from out of town flew down.

"H-h-hello. A-a-are you knitting a bill cozy?" asked the shivering puffin.

"I d-d-dropped mine passing through."

The puffin beamed with delight when Penguin gave it to him.

"Thank you!" said the grateful lovebirds.

The puffins hatched a secret plan to help the penguin find his own perfect match.

"What a perfect pair," thought Penguin.

"This bill cozy will make a nice hat," he said to the seal pup. "Wait here, and I'll knit you a scarf!"

On the other side of the ice, a cold visitor asked Bootsy for a favor.

"Could you knit me a sweater?" asked the whale. This was a BIG job, but Bootsy wanted to try.

When Bootsy reached for her basket, all her yarn was missing.

Penguin noticed his knitting box
was empty, too.

The penguins went on a search.

"Have you seen my yarn?" asked Bootsy.
"No," said Penguin. "I'm missing mine, too!"

Penguin and Bootsy set off to unravel the mystery together.

As they looked, they knitted for warmth.

They even knitted for friends along the way.

They knitted for fun.

They knitted for comfort.

And this made Penguin and Bootsy very happy, until . . .

. . . a blizzard came and
blew the penguins apart.

Their journeys were long and lonely.

Bootsy followed the trail through the rain

and snow   and dreamed of better days.

"I hope I will see you again," thought Penguin, as he laid out a sign for Bootsy to find.

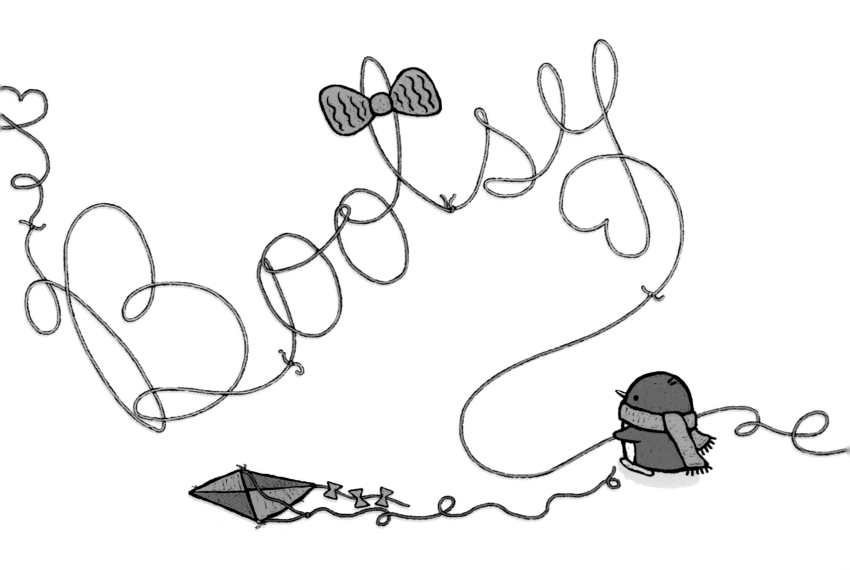

They knitted peak to peak as the trail of yarn went on and on. They pulled themselves up higher and higher.

Finally . . .

. . . they reached the very top.
Penguin and Bootsy had pulled
right into each other's hearts.

And together . . .

. . . love was a BIG adventure!

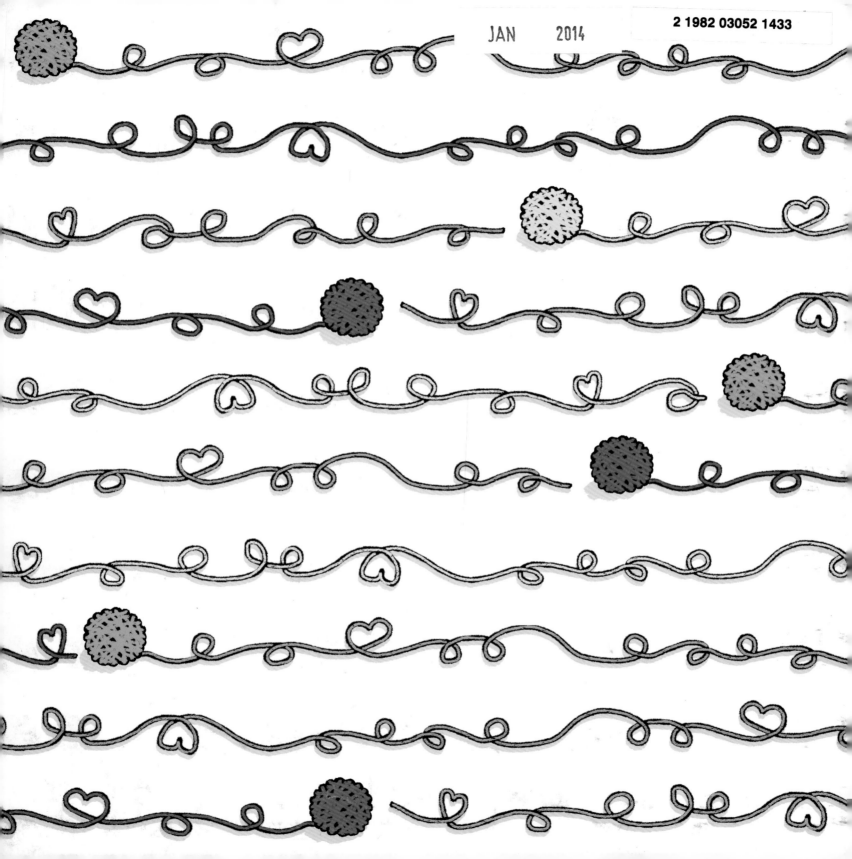